Mira had very **curly** hair. It **curled** at the front.
It **curled** at the back. It **curled** everywhere!

Mira didn't like her hair. She wanted it to be **STRAIGHT** and **SMOOTH**, just like her Mama's.

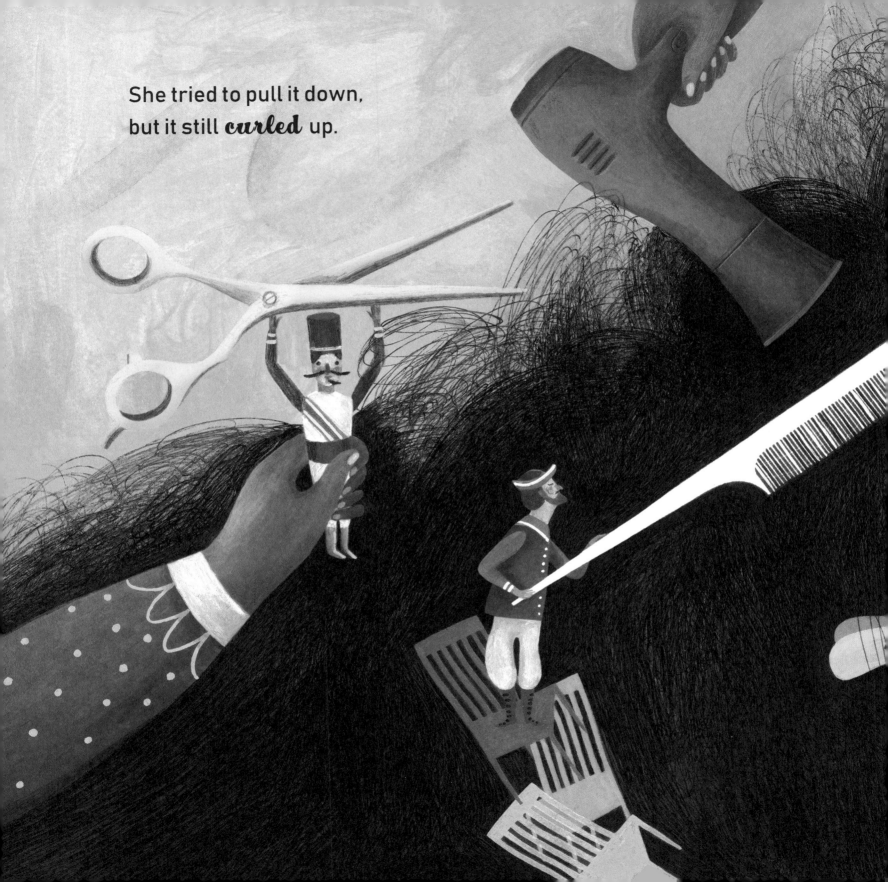

She tried to pull it down,
but it still *curled* up.

She stood on her head, but the *curling* wouldn't stop!

She used some old books

to STRAIGHTEN out her hair...

...but when she got up,

there were *curls* everywhere!

Mira wanted her hair to be

STRAIGHT

and

SMOOTH

just like her Mama's.

One cloudy day, Mira went for a stroll holding her Mama's hand.

Drip, drip, drip,

rain started to fall.

They ran towards
a palm areesh,

and crouched among
the chicks and geese.

As they sat waiting for
the rain to clear, Mira
looked at her Mama and
started to stare...

Mama's hair was *curling*! Up and up!
It kept on *curling*! It wouldn't stop!

"Mama! Mama! Look at your hair! It looks beautiful and free, *curling* everywhere!"

From that day on, *curls* were the only way Mira and her Mama wore their hair every day.